D0791995

Teen Life on Reservations and in First Nation Communities

Growing Up Native

Title List

Getting Ready for the Fair: Crafts, Projects, and Prize-Winning Animals

Growing Up on a Farm: Responsibilities and Issues

Migrant Youth: Falling Between the Cracks

Rural Crime and Poverty: Violence, Drugs, and Other Issues

Rural Teens and Animal Raising: Large and Small Pets

Rural Teens and Nature: Conservation and Wildlife Rehabilitation

Rural Teens on the Move:
Cars, Motorcycles, and Off-Road Vehicles

Teen Life Among the Amish and Other Alternative Communities:
Choosing a Lifestyle

Teen Life on Reservations and in First Nation Communities:
Growing Up Native

Teen Minorities in Rural North America: Growing Up Different

Teens and Rural Education: Opportunities and Challenges

Teens and Rural Sports: Rodeos, Horses, Hunting, and Fishing

Teens Who Make a Difference in Rural Communities:
Youth Outreach Organizations and Community Action

Teen Life on Reservations and in First Nation Communities
Growing Up Native

by Marsha McIntosh

Mason Crest Publishers

Philadelphia

Mason Crest Publishers Inc.
370 Reed Road
Broomall, Pennsylvania 19008
(866) MCP-BOOK (toll free)
www.masoncrest.com

First printing
1 2 3 4 5 6 7 8 9 10
ISBN 978-1-4222-0011-7 (series)

Library of Congress Cataloging-in-Publication Data

McIntosh, Marsha.
  Teen life on reservations and in First Nation communities : growing up
native / by Marsha McIntosh.
      p. cm. — (Youth in rural North America)
  Includes index.
  ISBN 978-1-4222-0018-6
  1. Indian teenagers—North America—Social life and customs—Juvenile
literature. 2. Indian reservations—North America—Juvenile literature. I.
Title. II. Series.
  E98.Y68M35 2007
  305.235089'97—dc22
                                      2006001466

Cover and interior design by MK Bassett-Harvey.
Produced by Harding House Publishing Service, Inc.
www.hardinghousepages.com

Cover image design by Peter Spires Culotta.
Cover photography by Kenneth McIntosh.
Printed in Malaysia by Phoenix Press.

Contents

Introduction

by Celeste Carmichael

Results of a survey published by the Kellogg Foundation reveal that most people consider growing up in the country to be idyllic. And it's true that growing up in a rural environment does have real benefits. Research indicates that families in rural areas consistently have more traditional values, and communities are more closely knit. Rural youth spend more time than their urban counterparts in contact with agriculture and nature. Often youth are responsible for gardens and farm animals, and they benefit from both their sense of responsibility and their understanding of the natural world. Studies also indicate that rural youth are more engaged in their communities, working to improve society and local issues. And let us not forget the psychological and aesthetic benefits of living in a serene rural environment!

The advantages of rural living cannot be overlooked—but neither can the challenges. Statistics from around the country show that children in a rural environment face many of the same difficulties that are typically associated with children living in cities, and they fare worse than urban kids on several key indicators of positive youth development. For example, rural youth are more likely than their urban counterparts to use drugs and alcohol. Many of the problems facing rural youth are exacerbated by isolation, lack of jobs (for both parents and teens), and lack of support services for families in rural communities.

When most people hear the word "rural," they instantly think "farms." Actually, however, less than 12 percent of the population in rural areas make their livings through agriculture. Instead, service jobs are the top industry in rural North America. The lack of opportunities for higher paying jobs can trigger many problems: persistent poverty, lower educational standards, limited access to health care, inadequate housing, underemployment of teens, and lack of extracurricular possibilities. Additionally, the lack of—or in some cases surge of—diverse populations in rural communities presents its own set of challenges for youth and communities. All these concerns lead to the greatest threat to rural communities: the mass exodus of the post–high school population. Teens relocate for educational, recreational, and job opportunities, leaving their hometown indefinitely deficient in youth capital.

This series of books offers an in-depth examination of both the pleasures and challenges for rural youth. Understanding the realities is the first step to expanding the options for rural youth and increasing the likelihood of positive youth development.

CHAPTER 1
Living on the Reservation— Living in Two Worlds

Trisha Ann Curley, age thirteen, is a full-blooded Navajo who is a part of a close-knit family. While she leads a full life involving school sports, vigorous studying that keeps her on the honor roll, and time to hang out with friends, she also has time for traditional Navajo ways. She was an Arizona State Finalist in the 2005 National American Miss Pageant in July of 2005. In the event of her winning, she planned the following words by Peggy Francis Scott to be part of her acceptance speech: "Harmony is when knowledge, feeling, and action are in balance."

At the center of Navajo belief is the need to be in harmony and right relationship, a Navajo term scholars translate as *beauty* in English. The Navajo world holds many opposites—male/female, bad/good, earth/sky—and the Navajo believe these opposites are needed for stability in the world. Each balances the other, and when things are in harmony there is good; when not, there is bad.

For young people like Trisha Ann Curley, achieving harmony between their Native traditions and North American culture can be a challenge. Growing up on a reservation means you must balance two worlds.

An Indian reservation in the United States is land that Native American tribes manage, in some cases under the U.S. Department of the Interior's Bureau of Indian Affairs. The U.S. government recognizes tribal lands as "sovereign nations," meaning that the federal government recognizes each tribe's right to make and enforce their own laws. Although there are more than five hundred recognized tribes, there are only about three hundred Indian reservations. Some tribes have more than one reservation, and some have none. Twelve reservations are larger than the state of Rhode Island, which is 776,960 acres (314,425 hectares), and nine are larger than the state of Delaware, which is 1,316,480 acres (532,761 hectares). Some states have no reservations.

People in the United States often refer to Native people as "Native Americans"; however, many Native people prefer the simple term "Indian." In Canada, most Native people are referred to as "First Nations"; however, Canadians do not call the Inuit and Metis groups First Nations people. The Inuit are Native peoples of the Canadian Arctic, and the Metis (pronounced MAY tee) are people descended from Cree, Ojibway, and Saulteaux women who married French Canadian and British settlers. Canadians call all three groups (First Nation peoples, Inuit, and Metis) "Aboriginal" or "First Peoples."

In Canada, a "First Nations reserve" is a *tract* of land the Queen has set apart for *indigenous* people, similar to Indian reservations

Native cultures find
beauty and harmony in
the natural world.

Because many Native teens live on isolated rural reservations, they enjoy festivals where they have a chance to celebrate their traditions with other North American Indians.

in the United States, although their histories are very different. Canadians also call them "Indian reserves," or "First Nation reserves." Some First Nation groups may occupy more that one reserve. The Indian Act gives the Minister of Indian Affairs the right to make sure that no one uses reserve land for any purpose than for the benefit of the Indians who live there. Government may only transfer the land title to the band or to individual members of the band. Neither Canadian nor U.S. governments tax Native lands or Native-owned property. There are over six million First Nation communities in Canada.

Teens on reservations and First Nations communities usually live in rural areas. Their lives are different from urban Native or urban Anglo people, not only because of the rural nature of their lives but also because of the rich traditions of their own cultures. However, the dominant culture may still have quite an effect on First Nation and Native American teens. Many of them attend schools run by federal governments, and they have contact with nearby cities. They have access to radio and television and in a sense live in two worlds.

This book tells the stories of various First Nations and Native American youth who balance their lives between two cultures. Ariel Rae Begaye, a Navajo and a fifth-generation weaver experienced *Kinaalda*, a traditional coming-of-age ceremony; she also enjoys playing basketball, listening to hip-hop, and participating in junior high school dances. Lucretia Birdinground from the Crow Nation reservation participates in the Crow Fair every year and uses her family sweat lodge several times a week; she likes all kinds of music from country to hip-hop, and her goal is to become a lawyer. Preston Parrish, a Navajo youth, lives for the rodeo, loves heavy metal music, and stays in shape by helping his grandmother herd sheep. Erinn Baptiste of the Algonquin First Nation loves school sports; her favorite traditional activity is attending the yearly Algonquin **powwow** and dancing the shawl dance, and in the summer, she works at the First Nation's museum as a storyteller.

Native teens enrich North America with their talents, skills, and ideas.

What do Native teens do for entertainment and fun, sports, and education? What are their traditions and beliefs? What are the challenges they face, and what are their hopes for the future? As you discover the answers to these questions, you will also discover all these teens have to offer North America.

CHAPTER 2
Art and Music

Twelve-year-old Ariel Rae Begaye sits patiently at her upright loom, intently weaving her braided twill rug. The yarn stretched up and down (the warp) is plain colored. She weaves the horizontal dyed yarn (the weft) back and forth between the warp. Thin wooden rods keep the warp in place, and Ariel uses a weaving comb to pack the wefts snugly over the warps to hide them. Weaving has surrounded Ariel since she was a child; she spent hours watching her grandmother and uncle at their looms and started her own weaving at the age of five. It takes her about one and a half months to make a small rug—if she works several hours each day.

Ariel's family are also weavers, so it's no wonder that weaving is important to this Native teen.

Ariel comes from a long line of weavers. Her grandmother, Mary K. Clah (also known as "Shima"), is a well-known third-generation master weaver. When Mary retired from weaving, she passed her tools and loom down to Roy, her son, as he was the only one of her children who was interested in the art. At the age of nine, he began to weave and kept up his interest during his teen years. Roy has inspired his sisters, nephews, and nieces to become involved in weaving as well. He often weaves with Ariel, helping her with her patterns and techniques. He raises his own churro sheep and dyes his own wool. The dyes come from plants, insects, and berries that he finds and processes. Then he shares his wool with his family, including his niece, Ariel.

No one is sure when and where the Navajo began weaving. Before the Spanish came, they were weaving cloth from wild cotton that grew in northern Arizona. The cotton grew in a head on the top of tall, wild grass. Many Navajo believe that Spiderwoman taught them to weave.

Ariel's family lives in the Teec Nos Pos area of Arizona, which is in the northeast near **Four Corners**. The Navajo Reservation has thirteen separate weaving regions, and each region has certain characteristics recognizable in their rugs. The designs in Navajo rugs do not have a specific religious meaning. Instead, each design is a unique creation of the weaver, and she keeps the design in her mind. Because Ariel is still young, her grandmother and her uncle help her with ideas for her designs and the colors of wool she should use.

One of the important lessons Ariel has learned from her uncle and grandmother is to neatly pack up her weaving material and tools when she is finished for the day. Another important lesson passed down by her grandma is to stop weaving when she becomes tired. Her grandma told her the legend of the Dine woman who wove too long.

The woman was homeless, so Spiderman and Spiderwoman made her a loom and taught her to weave, warning her not to weave too long at a time or she might lose herself in the weaving. But the woman did not pay attention to their advice. One day she wove and wove all night, and by the morning, she had woven herself into her rug. The people had to summon a medicine man to release her.

When Ariel is tired of weaving, she loves to play basketball and volleyball. She plays center position on a basketball team called the Lady Sparks, who have traveled to other states to play. She also gets plenty of practice playing basketball at home with her brother. She likes hip-hop music and going to dances at her Teec Nos Pos Middle School. Ariel hopes to one day be a surgeon. After her schooling, she wants to come back to the Navajo Reservation and live close to her mother and grandmother, or at least be within driving distance.

Ariel is one young person who is carrying on her people's tradition in a wonderful way. She hopes that other Dine youth will also become interested in the art.

Country Music on the Rez

Bineshi Albert, from Albuquerque, New Mexico's Sage Council, wrote on the Alternet Web site that music tastes among Indian youth are about the same as they were when he was in school. Youth have divided themselves into three camps—"the hip-hop crew, the cholo crew, and the headbanger/heavy metal crew"—but there is one more camp that some Native American teens belong to: the country music camp.

Connie Thompson, who lives in Polacca, Arizona, at the foot of First Mesa on the Hopi Reservation, has been a student at Hopi Junior/Senior High School for the last three years. Singing is one of her joys in life. For the 2004–2005 school year, Connie sang the National Anthem at the opening of every football and basketball game. This led to a very special invitation. Hearing her melodic voice, Wally Youvella Jr. asked her to sing with his group, a country band called Smoke Ring. Wally's father started the group several years ago, and it consists primarily of family members. Connie accepted the invitation and now spends many weekends performing at birthday parties, fund-raisers, an occasional battle of the bands, and

Creating beautiful works of art from yarn offers Native teens a wonderful sense of pride and achievement.

Native American dancers at the annual O'Odham Tash Powwow in Casa Grande have the chance to celebrate their culture while they have fun with others who share their traditions.

> "Music comes from the center of who we are. It gives an opportunity for your soul to speak, to be thankful and honest and to hopefully help other people along their journey."
>
> —George Leach

country dances. A mixture of young people and adults attend the dances. On July 30, 2005, the group released their first CD and had a dance at the Hopi Veterans Memorial Center to celebrate. A good crowd attended and danced the night away.

Dances are a welcome event with Hopi young people. There is not much to do in the way of entertainment on the three *mesas*, so dances, both religious and *secular*, are the most popular form of social activity. Hopi enjoy having a large party whenever family members have a birthday, graduation, homecoming from the army, or whenever there is any other reason to celebrate. Many times, they rent a hall and invite friends and relatives. "Come eat" is a common saying on the reservation. Sometimes they may roast a sheep, or have hot dogs, hamburgers, and salads. Often families will invite groups like Smoke Ring to entertain at these parties.

Connie is not Hopi, but she is part Native American. Her father is half Wichita and half Seneca Indian. Her mother is Anglo. The family lives on the Hopi Reservation because her father is the pastor of a church there. Her music is helping to keep Native tradition alive and growing in the twenty-first century.

Hip-hop offers Native teens a chance to express themselves.

Hip-Hop and Rap

A study called A Cappella North 2 surveyed many Canadian First Nation youth in the Yukon and found that 69 percent liked rap music best; hip-hop came second. Folk, world music, jazz, and classical were the least appreciated. Hip-hop rap has become very popular among many Native youth. Dave McLeod of NCI, Manitoba's Aboriginal radio station, says they have doubled their air time for the hip-hop show, Rez Nation.

McLeod believes that hip-hop rap gives First Nation teens a voice they would not have otherwise. Aboriginal rappers confront some

The group WARPARTY, a favorite with First Nation youth, was the winner of the 2001 Canadian Aboriginal Music Awards. The group's music encourages change and understanding between all people. Other favorite groups are Winnipeg's Slangblossom and Ontario's Tru Rez Crue.

tough issues in their music. They rap about land claims, residential schools, poverty, and racism. Alberta's hip-hop group WARPARTY told the Aboriginal Framework News Web site: "We're inspired by the stories from the reserves. People in the worst circumstances have had so much positive to say that they have inspired our songs. Those stories have helped us learn to let life move us." They are putting together a workshop called Dreams of Reality, to encourage kids to have dreams and not be discouraged by harsh realities. Hip-hop and rap now have their own category at the Aboriginal music awards.

Derek Edenshaw started rapping as a teen in 1995. Of Cree and Haida ancestry, Derek says the reason why Native teens have caught on to rap is simple: they have always had drums, and rap is a new adaptation of those drums and rhythms. Derek, also known as Manik, is a member of the British Columbia Aboriginal rap collective Tribal Wizdom. He started rapping at a Christmas talent show at his high school. He told the First Perspective Web site, "It was like a gift appeared out of nowhere."

Exploring one's own identity is a part of adolescence, whether a person is Native or not; it's a process that helps the individual make a successful transition into adulthood. For Native teens like Ariel

Powwows' dance and music connect Native young adults to their present community as well as their past heritage.

The Red Thunder Dancers

The Red Thunder Dancers are a group of youth from twelve to twenty years old who give their audiences an understanding of their Plains Indian traditions through songs, dance, and music. They perform dances such as the fancy shawl dance, the hoop dance (in which they re-create the eagle, bear, and buffalo), the jingle dress dance, and the prairie chicken dance. The dance troupe comes from the Tsuu T'ina First Nation near Calgary, and they have traveled across Canada and around the world. They have been to the Lincoln Center in New York City, the United Nations Children's Conference in New Zealand, and the National Geographic Conference in Lake Louise. The youngest Red Thunder Dancer placed in the top ten at the 2004 World Champion hoop dance competition in Phoenix, Arizona.

and Derek, music and art provide vital bridges that connect them to both their ancient traditions and the modern world, allowing them to express themselves. At the same time, they gain pride in their heritage and a sense of self-worth.

And besides, art and music are just plain fun. And so are sports, another source of Native identity and pride.

CHAPTER 3
Sports, Sports, Sports

Sports changed the life of Trisha Ann Curley, a full-blooded Navajo who lives in Tuba City on the Navajo Reservation. Before she played sports, Trisha was heading in a negative direction. Her mother made her change schools to Tuba City Boarding School, where the coaches noticed how tall and strong Trisha was and encouraged her to get involved in sports. She played junior varsity basketball and was on the track and field team in seventh grade; she earned six ribbons and placed in every meet in the shot put and discus events. "I got straightened out, I never won awards before," says Trisha. "The kids who make positive choices are people who are involved in sports. When you do sports you run around and sweat out all of your problems, it helps out." She believes that sports make people feel good about themselves. Sports build confidence and give kids positive things to do.

First Nation Sports

For thousands of years before Europeans arrived on the continent, Aboriginal nations participated in games. Historical records support the belief that many modern-day team sports came from these Aboriginal games. Historians believe these games contributed to social values and personal character qualities such as honesty, respect for elders, courage, personal excellence, and acceptance of elder leadership—qualities found in the lifestyle of Native peoples. Throughout Indian reservations and First Nation communities across North America, sports are still important to many Native young people today.

Basketball is one of those sports. Sariah Two Leggins is a star basketball player on the Lady Bull Dogs team at the Crow Reservation's high school in Hardin, Montana. According to *Christian Science Monitor* writer, Todd Wilkinson, Sariah is a shy athlete who, in the opinion of her school counselor, is a role model for other Crow teens. She is one teen who has decided to abstain from alcohol and has set her goal to attend college after high school. Sariah comes from a long line of people who love basketball.

Larry Colton, author of *Counting Coup*, describes Sharon LaForge, another star basketball player from the Lady Bull Dogs team. Colton found that high school basketball players were often the heroes of the Crow tribe, and often the best players in the state of Montana. Larry followed Sharon through her senior year with all of the joys of winning games alongside the difficulties in her personal life.

Many Native young people are excited about basketball.

Sharon had an intense love of basketball: it was her life, something she naturally was good at but that she also worked hard at. Meanwhile, she struggled with normal teenage pressures such as peer group troubles, finding her place in life, and dating problems, and she also faced problems that are special to teens living on reservations. In the end, Sharon triumphed over many odds.

Football in Navajo Nation

One look at the living room wall of Nicholas Curley, Trisha Ann's brother, and you know that football is one of the loves of his life. The

Curley family has pictures of Nicholas with a football in his hand at different ages scattered among the family wall of pictures. Videos of his games, recorded by his father, Allen, line the shelf above their big-screen TV. Allen, who also was a high school football player, attends every game Nicholas plays. Allen does not just attend however; he makes the most noise of any fan. A homemade device, a cluster of loud cowbells, can be heard coming from Allen's part of the stands during the Tuba City Junior High School games, whether they're at home or away in other towns.

Nicholas has played various football positions throughout his middle school years. As a freshman, Nicholas played quarterback for the Tuba City High School Braves in the 2005–2006 school year. He practices hard, plays hard, and is an honor to his family and to those who have come before him in the world of Indian football.

Ontario Aboriginal Summer Games

On July 14–17 of 2005, Native young people from all over Ontario, Canada, met at the Laurentian University in the town of Sudbury for the Ontario Aboriginal Summer Games. Teams participated in track and field, basketball, and tae kwon do competitions. This was not simply a yearly competition; this was an event where scouts would be looking for the best athletes to put on Team Ontario, which would go to the 2006 North American Indigenous Games in Denver, Colorado.

The North American Indigenous Games were created to give the United States and Canada an opportunity to gather together to compete and share in cultural activities. Three thousand athletes attended the first games, held in Edmonton, Canada; by 1997, 8,000 participants gathered in Victoria, Canada. During the competition, every province, territory, and state in Canada and the United States competes in sixteen sports: 3-D archery, athletics (track), bad-

Lacrosse is a truly Native sport; not only is it popular with many modern-day Native American teens, but it was also first played by the tribes of the Northeast.

Rodeo events are another sport popular with many Native young people.

> "The most popular sports on the reservation today are modern. Long noted for their expertise as equestrians, the Crow have many excellent rodeo riders. Basketball is also immensely popular, especially at the level of high school competition. Although these games lack traditional roots, they help to bind the tribe together into a cohesive and meaningful unit."
>
> —Kenneth McIntosh, <u>North American Indians Today: Crow.</u>

minton, baseball, basketball, boxing, canoeing, golf, field lacrosse, rifle shooting, soccer, softball, swimming, tae kwon do, volleyball, and wrestling. Three are traditional sports, and thirteen are nontraditional.

The Algonquins of Pikwakanagan looked forward to the July 2005 event for months. The community hired a coach to work with their boys. The Algonquin team played other teams from around Canada to get practice and to give the scouts more opportunities to watch the players.

Danielle Meness, an assistant with Brighter Futures Program, says that basketball is the most popular sport in their community. Some teens also enjoy lacrosse, and a few play hockey. All gain a sense of pride, connection, and most of all, fun.

CHAPTER 4
Rodeo and Outdoor Sports

The sun is shining, action music is playing, and there is an electric atmosphere as fans watch cowboy after cowgirl do the barrel race, ride a bull, rope a calf, and do some ribbon roping. It is summertime in Navajo land, and rodeos rule almost every weekend in many towns across the reservation from spring until fall. Not only do adults compete but also many young people. Junior rodeos are a popular attraction.

Young Cowboys

Bull riding is a favorite among rodeo spectators, perhaps because it is so dangerous. The rider must stay on the bull for a full eight seconds. Judges award extra points to a rider when he can steer the bull on a straight course and keep the proper posture during his bumpy ride.

Bull riding is a favorite sport for Preston Parrish, a thirteen-year-old from the town of Kayenta on the Navajo Reservation. While some youth start their bull riding careers by first riding sheep, Preston's first ride was at the age of eight on the back of a bull. He watched many hours of videos of his dad and uncles riding bulls to get ready for his first ride, learning what to do and how to stay on the back of a bull. His dad and uncles worked with him to train him. Preston is currently a member of the Western Junior Rodeo Association. He often rides with his thirteen-year-old uncle, Landon Parrish, in rodeo events.

Preston stays in shape and practices between rodeos. He practices on the barrel, lifts weights two times a week, and runs three times a week up hard sand hills by his house. He also helps his grandma herd sheep.

And there's a lot of running involved in herding sheep. In the morning, Preston's grandma lets the sheep out of the pen to graze. During the day, they wander a long distance. In the evening, someone has to go and round them up and put them in their pen. Sometimes the sheep dog does the work, but when he is too lazy to herd sheep, Preston steps in and runs to find them.

In one of the first rodeos of the 2003–2004 Arizona Junior Rodeo Association's season, a bull named Elmer gave Preston one of his most memorable rides. When the gate opened, Elmer made a couple of jumps into the ring, spun to the right, and went three rotations, came out of the spin, and ran straight. Preston scored seventy-two points and took third place.

Bull riding can be dangerous. An ambulance is kept waiting at one of the gates at any rodeo. A bull injured Preston at a rodeo in the town of Kayenta. When the gate opened, the bull took one big jump to the right, Preston went too far forward, and the bull hit him in the head. Preston had to get eight stitches above his left eye, but he was back riding bulls in a week.

Bull riding is an exciting—and dangerous—sport.

A Navajo boy's rodeo boots are powerful symbols of hope and pride.

A History of Excellence in the Rodeo

- Three Persons of Alberta, Canada, was an early Canadian Native rodeo star who won the World Bucking Horse Championship at the first Calgary Stampede in 1912, winning over many experienced Anglo cowboys in the area.

- Jackson Sundown (Nez Pierce) was one of the best known of the early Indian cowboys in the United States. After age forty, he began competing professionally. He won the World Championship in 1916.

The Parrish family has not always lived on the reservation. Last year, Preston lived in Phoenix. This year, though, his family moved back to the reservation to be close to relatives, and Preston now attends Kayenta Middle School. Preston enjoys the special freedom he has on the Navajo Reservation. He can run to stay in shape any time he wants, and hills and **washes** provide more challenging places to run. In Phoenix, a nightly curfew restricted his training, and the only place to run was on flat, hard surfaces.

Not surprisingly, *8 Seconds* is Preston's favorite movie. It is the story of world champion Lane Frost, a bull rider who lost his life participating in the sport. His other heroes are rodeo riders Ty Murray, Tuff Hedeman, Jim Sharp, Michael Gaffney, and Cody Lambert—all riders in the Professional Bull Riders Association. His favorite fun activity on the reservation is hopping on bulls and steers. Preston's goal is to be a world champion in rodeo—he wants to ride horses as well as bulls, and he wants to be the best.

Justin Granger is another Navajo bull rider. His father is the president of the Junior Bull Riders Association. Justin practices riding every week at the junior bull rider's arena outside of Tuba City. Getting a good night's sleep is one way Justin makes sure he is in good shape to ride at a rodeo competition.

The Navajo have a long tradition of ranching and rodeos. Soon after the Spanish brought horses, sheep, and cattle to the Southwest, Navajos began to herd, and today's Indian cowboys have been raising and *breaking* horses for years. Though no one knows when the first Navajo rodeo began, it certainly grew out of the friendly competitions that arose from everyday ranching activities. Informal competitions were common for generations before rodeos started.

Competitions began on reserves and in local communities. As rodeo became a sport in the 1950s, Indian rodeo associations began organizing around the United States and Canada. Today, over twenty Native Plains and Plateau rodeo associations are in the United States, the largest in the Southwest. In Canada, there are five Native Plains and Plateau rodeo associations. From the Esketemc First Nation People in British Colombia, Canada, to the Plains Indians of the United States, rodeos are a much-loved activity.

Indian rodeos differ somewhat from other rodeos. On the surface they may seem the same, but one of the biggest differences is the respect the Indians have for the animals, a respect that comes from Natives' long-standing relationship with supernatural and natural beings. Some Native Americans see horses and cattle as the modern-day buffalo. Many rodeos begin with a cowboy prayer and then a prayer in a Native language. The cowboy acknowledges that the animals are superior to him and asks them not to be too hard on the humans competing.

Rodeos offer young participants a sense of achievement and identity.

Native rodeos also have children's events and sometimes community events that other rodeos might not have. Native participants are proud to be able to perform in front of their friends and families.

Skiing and Snowboarding

Native Voices Foundation co-chair, Olympic skier, Suzie Chaffee, is trying to raise awareness all over the United States of the need to assist Native youth with their skiing efforts. The benefits of skiing are many for youth on reservations with snow. For example, the White

Snowboarding is a popular Native sport, especially in northern states and territories.

Mountain Apache have the highest employment rate of any reservation, thanks in large part to their skiing. As reported on the Native Voices Foundation Web site, chairman Dallas Masey said that skiing is the number-one motivator for their youth. When Apache teens become involved with skiing at a young age, they are also less likely to abuse alcohol.

Native Voices Foundation is looking to jumpstart Native youth to be able to compete in the Olympics as *sovereign nations*. First Nations have received $3 million from Vancouver's Organizing Olympic Committee to train snowboarders across Canada for the

Callan Chythlook-Sifsof, a fifteen-year-old Yup'ik living at Alyeska Ski Resort in Alaska, proudly won the 2005 Junior Olympic Snowboard Championships in Jackson Hole, Wyoming.

2010 Olympics. The money came after the government of Canada apologized to their First Nations for broken treaties, removals, and abusive government boarding schools. The Canadian government gave the $3 million as a healing fund.

In 2005, many U.S. citizens became aware of the plight of Indian youth when a teenager on Minnesota's Red Lake Reservation killed nine people and then himself at school. Many Native youth feel hopeless. Native youth have a suicide rate higher than any other race in America, and the rate was the same 120 years ago. The effects of removals from their lands, being sent to boarding schools where their culture was squelched, and broken treaties are still being felt today. According to the National Voices Foundation, a Senate study found that "American Indians are still too depressed . . . and have the highest unemployment in America."

Chaffee believes that if people across America will chip in to help connect one hundred ski areas for Native youth, focusing first on the Red Lake Reservation, it will help to "lift their spirits, and restore their joy, health, and productivity."

Whether it's skiing, basketball, or some other sport, athletics are undoubtedly good for Native teens. Tex Hall, president of the National Congress of the American Indians, said, "Indian youth sports opportunities are the answer."

CHAPTER 5
Traditions and Beliefs

Erinn Baptiste, a sixteen-year-old from the Canadian First Nations Algonquins of Pikwakanagan, loves her nation's tradition of powwows. Every year the Algonquins are host to approximately 10,000 visitors who come to see them put on their *regalia* and celebrate their culture. For Erinn and other teens in the Algonquin nation, this is the most exciting event on the First Nation's calendar.

Canadian First Nation Powwows

Erinn is a shawl dancer. Her costume is burgundy red, and she wears a colorful shawl with a fringe that whirls as she moves her arms up and down and around rhythmically to the drum beat. She learned the dance from her friends. At powwows, she learns new steps from new friends. In August of 2005, Erin had the opportunity to have a new outfit for her dancing. The nation's leaders obtained a grant with enough money so that everyone in the nation may buy material to make new outfits.

Dancing is only part of the fun of powwows for Erinn. Meeting teens from other First Nation communities is another highlight. During these gatherings, Erinn camps out with her friends. They have good times sharing fun and conversation as they connect through their cultural heritage.

One of the cultural delights at almost all powwows is the food. Indian tacos are a favorite of many people. **Fry bread** about the size of a dinner plate is the basis of the taco, and layered on top are chili, lettuce, tomatoes, and cheese. Erinn has another favorite powwow food—beaver tail—but not the kind that was once attached to an animal. A beaver tail is a scone topped with cinnamon and sugar.

Crow Fair

The Crow Nation has hosted a powwow since 1904. The Crow word for it is *Um-basax-bilua,* which means, "where they make noise." Eighteen-year-old Lucretia Birdinground looks forward to the event every year during the third week in August. Her family joins the rest of the nation in camping out in tepees along the Little Bighorn River. More than 1,500 tepees are set up each year—so it's no wonder Crow Fair is known as the "Te-pee Capital of the World."

The fair began when **Indian agent** S. C. Reynolds tried to get the Crow Nation more interested in farming. He suggested that they hold a fair each year to show off their cattle and vegetables. To stir up more interest, he suggested they hold their traditional dances and ceremonies at the same time. As time went on, the Crow dropped the agricultural aspect of the event.

Native teens at a powwow in Arizona show off their beautiful costumes.

Dancing in a drum circle unites Native Americans to each other and to their traditions.

Today, the fair begins with a parade of colorfully dressed people on floats, trucks, cars, and horses. Judges award cash prizes for the different categories in the parade. An important part of the parade is the six powwow princesses chosen from the six districts of the reservation. The district of Reno chose Lucretia as their princess in 2003.

The grand entry signals that the dances are about to begin. An honor guard of military veterans carrying flags leads the procession, followed by men's and then women's fancy, grass, and traditional dancers.

Fancy dances are somewhat new to powwows. Dressed in bright colors with shiny outfits and dyed feather bustles, these dancers show off their athletic skills and timing. Meanwhile, traditional dancers step with pride and purpose. Male dancers wear bone breastplates, fur or feather headdresses, and feather bustles. Women traditional dancers wear buckskin dresses that are beaded and fringed. They wear fur-braided wraps and eagle feathers in their hair. All the dance movements have meaning.

The dance competitions have different categories. Contest dances are judged, and money prizes are given. Exhibition dances demonstrate different traditions of tribes, and for those who want to join the dance, there are intertribal dances.

During the six-day event, people enjoy reuniting with relatives and friends who live off the reservation. A quarter of the 10,000 Crows live in other parts of the country, making the fair a grand social time of laughing, talking, and playing games. Thousands of visitors from other Native nations, as well as Anglos, come to watch the event. Other Indian nations bring jewelry, pottery, and other goods to sell.

Besides the dancing and parades, there are rodeos and horse racing to enjoy. And no one starves at the fair; there is lots of delicious food. Lucretia loves the delicious Indian tacos, beaver tail, and the other favorite food at the Crow nation—menudo, Crow style. The secret ingredient is buffalo *tripe*.

Honor Dance

To hear someone tell another person how wonderful you are is a very pleasant feeling. Passing on the good news about a wonderful family member is a powwow tradition, done in the form of an Honor Dance. During the dance, a relative may tell the audience of an individual's accomplishments. If it is a child, the dance may tell about her good grades, extracurricular activities, compassionate nature, and kindness to her family. The relative will then invite the audience to come and shake hands and congratulate the family members as they follow the daughter while she dances around the circle. As the audience comes forward, they will usually drop a feather, sage, sweet grass, tobacco, or money in a container held by the leader. Then they fall in with the family until a crowd follows behind the honored person.

After the procession has circled the field, the family awards gifts to specific people. If there are drum circles, they may give them a gift for the group such as a cooler on wheels. Other gifts may include blankets and cases of soda. The gift-giving continues as the family walks around the field again, passing out baggies of school supplies, crayons, coloring books, and notebooks to the junior members of the audience. What a way to let the world know how proud you are of someone!

Storytelling

When visitors tour the museum at the Algonquin of Pikwakanagan community, they will hear Erinn Baptiste, sixteen, tell a traditional story. Storytelling is a good way to pass on traditions and to teach wisdom and character qualities.

One day the great Creator was making animals one at a time. He tried to make each animal just the way they asked him to. When it

Totem poles in British Columbia portray the beliefs and traditions of the Tlingit people.

A Nez Percé sweat lodge is a simple shelter made from bent branches. Many Native groups find spiritual, physical, and emotional healing from participating in sweat lodge ceremonies.

was Rabbit's turn, he asked to have the longest legs and ears in the world. The Creator made long, soft ears and long back legs, but just as he was working on the front legs, owl interrupted him.

Owl went on and on about how he wanted to look. The Creator kept telling him to be quiet, but he owl went on rudely talking. Finally, the Creator became very angry.

"You want colorful feathers? Yours will be grey and brown!" The Creator rubbed Owl in the mud. "You want a graceful neck? You will have no neck!" And he pushed Owl's head into his body. "You want

Sweat Lodges

One of Lucretia Birdinground's favorite traditions on the Crow Reservation is the sweat lodge. Her family has one in their backyard, and her father "builds a sweat" two times a week. Friends and relatives come join them. The men go in first and spend about an hour. Then the women go in.

Crows link much symbolism to the sweat lodge. As a religious ceremony progresses inside, a participant raises the door flap each of the four times he says a prayer. The sweat is for two purposes: to show devotion to the Creator and to purify the body by removing harmful substances. Lucretia uses it many times for relaxation, but she always ends her time with prayer.

beautiful eyes? You will have big eyes that only see in the night! You want to sing the nicest song? You will hoot the rest of your days!" And so the Great Creator made the owl one of the strangest looking birds in the world."

When Rabbit saw how angry the Creator was, he was so afraid that he ran away before the Creator could finish his front legs. With his little short front legs and long back legs, Rabbit had to hop everywhere—and he never got over his nervousness.

A young Native girl finds a sense of identity and affirmation in her cultural traditions.

Kinaalda

Ariel Begaye ran a special race when she was nine years old. When she reached the finish line, she was a Navajo woman.

The race was part of a ceremony called Kinaalda, a coming-of-age ceremony for Navajo girls. Although many things have changed in the lives of the Navajo people, their ceremonies have altered very little. The Kinaalda has been part of Navajo girls' lives for many generations. Traditionally, a girl is ready to have the ceremony when she has had her first menstrual cycle.

The Navajos believe the Kinaalda helps girls understand what life is like as a woman. It teaches her about her culture and the respon-

In Apache and Navajo tradition, Changing Woman is an earth-goddess, the daughter of Dawn and Darkness. She constantly transforms herself, so she always stays young.

sibilities she has to her family. Many relatives help with the event, but the ultimately the success of the Kinaalda is up to the girl herself.

According to Navajo tradition, the first Kinaalda was created for White Shell Woman, who later became Changing Woman, an individual who lives at the heart of Navajo culture. The Kinaalda was done for White Shell Woman so that she could have children. It is now done for Navajo women so that they too will be fertile and have children.

In his book *Kinaalda: A Navajo Girl Grows Up*, author Monty Roessel describes the traditional Kinaalda. It usually takes place in a hogan, a traditional Navajo house. The ceremony begins with the girl's mother brushing her daughter's hair with a grass brush. She ties her daughter's hair back with a piece of buckskin, but leaves her bangs to fall across her face. The girl cannot wear any makeup. After this, the family sings the first prayer in Navajo, the same prayer that was sung at the very first Kinaalda. Then the girl changes into a traditional dress. She wears a **concho** belt, heavy turquoise necklaces, and buckskin moccasins that extend up her calves.

After dressing, the girl lays down on a palate of buckskin and blankets. People have placed car keys, wallets, shawls, pictures, and necklaces between the blankets, hoping that some of the blessings from the prayers will also affect them. This ceremony, as with others, is not only for the "patient" as the person is called, but also for the spectators. A *medicine man* serves as a doctor for the ceremony.

As the girl lies down, the mother of the girl begins "molding" her, shaping her into a beautiful, strong woman. When she is done, she squeezes her daughter's stomach so she will not get fat. The spectators then line up, and the girl molds them; sometimes people request her to touch their sore back or arm, hoping for relief from pain.

After the molding, the girl runs out of the hogan toward the east, followed by the people who received the molding, shouting "Oooyiiee!" Running toward the east is important, because the Navajo believe that all things begin in the east. The young girl will run every day of her ceremony, once in the morning and once during the afternoon. The ceremony traditionally runs four days, but modern Navajos sometimes shorten it to two days because of job schedules.

After the first run, the girl returns to the hogan to make a special cake. This is the most important part of the ceremony. The young woman has to sew cornhusks together to make a cover for the cake. When she is finished, she has made a four-foot (1.2-meter) round crust cover for her cake. Her aunt breaks the news that she now has to make another one just like it. The women in her family cover the hole in the ground with paper bags and a cornhusk cover, and the other husk cover is put on top. Then the girl blesses the cake. Everyone who is at the ceremony takes a turn blessing the cake. They put paper bags on top of the cake, and then dirt is spread on top.

Someone lights the fire again, and now the young girl must stay awake all night while prayers are sung introducing her to the Holy People. The hope is that they will protect her on her journey through life. Community and family members help during the night to keep the fire going. They pray with the medicine man all night.

Everyday things—like blankets and cakes—take on spiritual significance in many Native cultures. This beautiful blanket was handwoven by a Navajo weaver.

Meanwhile, the girl goes into the hogan to spend the night. She must sit with her legs outstretched in front of her and her back straight. This is not easy to do for the whole night. Right before dawn, she finally gets to stretch her legs. Someone pulls back the blanket over the door, and the girl runs out of the hogan. People run behind her, breaking the silence of the night with the sounds of shoes hitting the ground. In a little while, the girl returns and runs back into the hogan, wrapped in a colorful blanket. The runners go in with her, but all is quiet; the prayers are over now.

The coming of the dawn means that she is almost a woman. The family hurries outside to cut the cake. If the cake is not done, according to tradition, the girl will have a hard life. When the cake is

Changing Woman is a powerful role model for Native young women.

cut, the center pieces are saved for special people at the ceremony. The center is the holiest part of the cake. After her ceremony, the young woman may not look different, but she is now considered a woman.

When asked what was different about her life after the ceremony, Ariel said others expect her to behave in a more mature way now: to act as Changing Woman would. At social gatherings, she can no longer run around with the other boys and girls; she is now a woman.

The ceremony reminds girls to take care of themselves and to be aware of the blessings of women's duties. Some families find that the ceremony is very expensive. The cost of a medicine man is high, many families give gifts to the friends and family who come, and the cost of outfitting the girl is also expensive. Nevertheless, it is a wonderful way to affirm a girl's identity and power.

Traditions like these connect Native youth to the larger community, to their past, and to a sense of themselves. In a larger culture that is often unsympathetic if not destructive, traditions play an important role. They help Indian teens know who they are and how they fit into the world.

CHAPTER 6
Education

"If it hadn't been for my school, I don't think I would be where I am in life right now," says Lucretia Birdinground. Lucretia is from the Crow Nation and has grown up on the Crow Reservation in southern Montana. She graduated in 2005 from St. Labre High School and is looking forward to college. Her plans are to attend the community college on the reservation, Little Big Horn College, then transfer to Bozeman State University to get her degree in business administration, and go on for a law degree.

Before she went to St. Labre High School, Lucretia did not believe in herself and her abilities as much as she does now. The teachers there were compassionate and dedicated, and very involved with the students' lives. They helped Lucretia learn to believe in herself and pushed her to her limits.

Several types of schools exist in First Nations communities and on Native American reservations. If the reserve is large enough, it may have national government-run schools, schools operated by the Native nation, and privately run institutions usually connected to a church. According to Indian and Northern Affairs Canada, "There are currently 502 schools on reserve, all but 8 are under First Nation management." St. Labre is an example of a private Catholic school in the United States.

George Yoakum had a hand in the founding of St. Labre. As a soldier stationed in Montana in 1884, he saw the devastation many Indians faced because of *homesteading*. He contacted the Montana bishop, told him of the homelessness and suffering, and asked if the church could help. The bishop purchased land and started St. Labre School in Ashland, Montana, on the edge of the Northern Cheyenne Reservation. Today it has an enrollment of 800 on three campuses, including Pretty Eagle Catholic School at St. Xavier and St. Charles Mission School at Pryor, on the Crow Reservation.

The people at St. Labre believe education changes lives and every child has a right to a good education. The school advertises that it brings together the finest resources, professional expertise, and a sense of commitment to give a quality education to everyone they serve. The curriculum includes classes in Native American language and culture.

Students who live more than forty miles (64.4 kilometers) away have the opportunity to stay in a dorm at St. Labre. Lucretia loved dorm life. She learned responsibility by having chores to do, since the students all had to help keep the common areas in the dorm clean.

Two First Nation girls take pride in their school and in their friendship with each other.

Native American teens enjoy the chance to socialize at an after-school activity.

Every morning the students had to be up by seven. They ate breakfast, did their chores, and were in classes by eight. After school, they had free time until dinner at 5:30. Homework time was between 6:30 and 7:30, followed by free time until 9:30, when they had fifteen minutes of prayers before bedtime at 10:00.

Lucretia was fortunate to be one of two students picked to be foreign exchange students from St. Labre. Two students from a Native tribe in Argentina, called the Mapuche, came to St. Labre. They got a feel for the culture in Ashland, Montana, and talked of their own lives and culture back in Argentina. All four students then took a trip to Washington, D.C. After that, the Argentinean girls went with Lucretia and her partner from the Northern Cheyenne Reservation

Interesting Facts

Root beer, syringes, rubberized clothing, freeze-dried food, and beef jerky are a few of the inventions and discoveries that Native people gave to the world. Indian healers discovered many of the pharmaceuticals we use today hundreds of years before Europeans reached the American shores.

to their town of Junin de Los Andes, where the North American girls shared their culture with the community. Lucretia wore a Crow traditional dress and did a traditional dance. The Northern Cheyenne student danced the fancy shawl dance; the Mapuche tribe also danced one of their traditional dances. Lucretia thought it looked something like a tango dance. The experience of traveling to another country and culture expanded Lucretia's knowledge of the world and other cultures.

Education at the Hopi Reservation

For years, the people of the Hopi Reservation in the United States had been pushing to bring the education of their children close to home so they would no longer have to go far away to boarding schools. In *The People: Indians of the American Southwest*, Stephan Tremble tells how in 1986, Hopi Junior/Senior High School opened its doors between Second and Third mesa. It is a federally funded Bureau of Indian Affairs school, but the board consists of local Hopi members. One of the focuses of the school is to provide a chance for students to be more involved in cultural activities. Having the school so close to home gives parents the opportunities to be more involved in the lives of their young people. For centuries, Pueblo parents have passed their culture down through the everyday activities of life. Young people ask questions, parents respond, and the culture is preserved. Hopi High enables this tradition to continue within the realm of more formal education.

The school has approximately 750 students. Since the Navajo Reservation surrounds the Hopi Reservation, and because the junior/senior high school has a good reputation, some Navajo attend as well, and the children of Anglo teachers and other workers on the reservation also attend. Students come as far away as an hour's driving time, and in the winter, snow and ice are a problem.

The students dress much like anywhere else in the United States—in blue jeans. The one difference a person might notice is that most everyone on the school campus is dressed very modestly. This is not because the administration has demanded it (there was no dress code prior to 2005), but because that is the preference of most of the students. One teen commented that the students mix together well. A student who wears black Goth outfits might play on the football team. Likewise, a "jock" basketball player might be heavily involved in the art program at school. There seems to be more of a blending of students instead of definite lines between interest groups. At times, however, feelings of rivalry can rise up between mesas.

During weekends when ceremonial dances are scheduled, the administration lets students out of school on Friday to help prepare for them. The dances rotate between First, Second, and Third Mesa, so not all of the students are out at once.

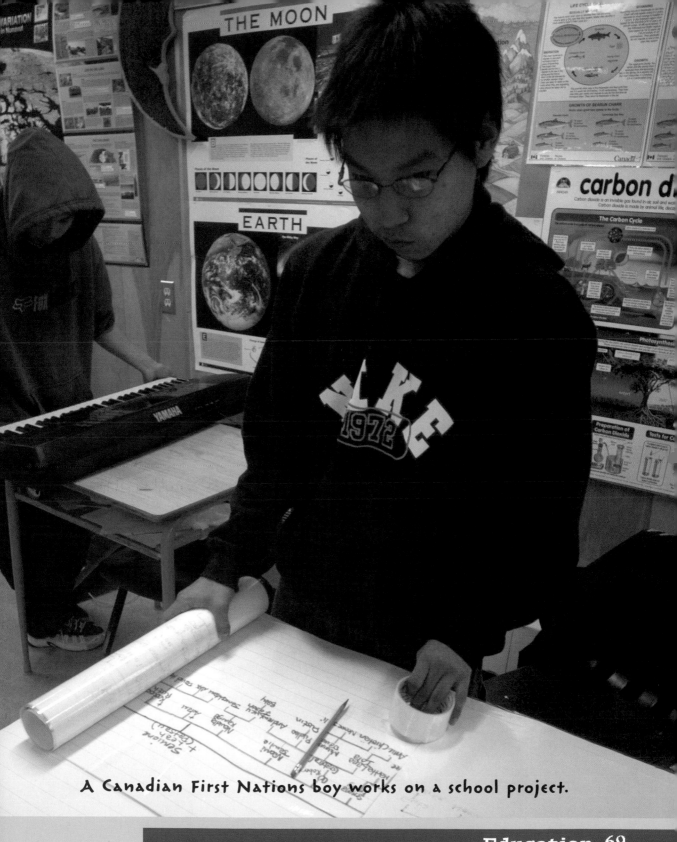

A Canadian First Nations boy works on a school project.

First Nation schools are based on the belief that education is a life-long process.

The Hopi schools place a high priority on culture and language. Over the years, however, there have been conflicts over which dialect to teach at the high school, since each mesa has its own language variations.

First Nation Education

Many First Nation people have been calling for change in Canada's educational system. They want to have total ownership of the education of their youth. In May of 2005, the Assembly of First Nations met and reconfirmed their desire to have full control and power over the education of their children. There are many reasons for this.

For one thing, First Nation people have a different view of education. They believe that it is a life-long process, beginning in the cradle and continuing into old age. The elders and women in their communities are the ones who pass down the culture to the younger generation; therefore, they need to have a part in the education of their youth. They believe that First Nation language and cultural values must be the foundation of their education if they are to have success in educating their youth.

In 2004, Canada's auditor general found that there is a wide educational gap between First Nation people who live on the reserve and other Canadians. As of 2005, out of 120,000 students in reserve schools from grades K through 12, only 32 percent are graduating. The results are the same for First Nation students attending provincial schools. The auditor general also found that the gap is widening. Some believe that change will only come when First Nation communities are fully in charge of their own schools.

The Na Cho Nyak Dun in British Columbia is one community that is pressing the territorial and federal government to transfer educational control to their nation. They want to start a new program based on the values of their culture. The Na Cho Nyak Dun believe that such a program would help their youth to have more pride, self-esteem, and dignity. The program would continue to use British Columbia curriculum but would also include Na Cho Nyak Dun culture, language, and history.

The regional director general for the Department of Indian Affairs and Northern Development told the *Whitehorse Daily Star Online* that she knows how difficult it is when negotiating education issues, since they go to the heart of a community. She does not think that it makes much sense to divide the territory into separate educational hub; while she concedes that working out this educational control issue will be a challenge for everyone, she feels that it can also be a learning experience.

Canada's federal government points out that if large territories struggle to meet all the needs of students in the public school system, how will small communities be able to meet them? It is a huge job for a small group to take on, but many First Nation communities want the challenge and the freedom.

Other Forms of Education

Erinn Baptiste is from the Algonquins of Pikwakanagan, a small community in Ontario. All of the youth in this community go to nearby towns for school, but Erinn loves her high school of about 300 students. She says many teens do not like school, but she would rather be there than just sitting at home. In the winter, she plays broomball (a game much like hockey but played with a broom), and in the spring, she competes in track and field events. She plays baseball in the summer, and in the fall, she runs cross-country. Other sports offered at her school are basketball, hockey, badminton, golf, and soccer. Of all the sports, however, the favorite at the school is rugby.

When she is not playing sports, Erinn is an educator herself—but not at school. She has a summer job at the Manido Chiman Museum

Inuit and First Nation students in Nunavut, Canada, enjoy the opportunity to learn together.

First Nation teens in Nunavut, Canada, work together on a school assignment.

in her First Nation's community as one of the storytellers. Any Algonquin youth who has reached ninth grade may have a summer job in the Algonquin community. It is a bit of an education just getting the job, however. Young people must fill out a formal application, make a resume, write an appropriate cover letter, and go before an interview panel of three people. After the interview—whether or not the youth got the job—an adult coaches them on their job application skills, and the youth receives pointers on how she could do better. The hope is that by the time the teen is out of school and applying for jobs in any community, she will be well prepared for the application process.

Danielle Meness is also helping to prepare Algonquin youth for the future. She works as an assistant with the Brighter Futures Program, a program for all ages. Among other things, she helps to run a summer program for youths. The parents pay one dollar a day for the program, and the summer staff involve the kids in interesting activities five days a week for six weeks. One of the reasons Danielle enjoys working with the Brighter Futures Program is because it is always changing. At the beginning of every year, a team circulates around the Algonquin community and talks with every member about the needs of the group. The program leaders then base the next year's programs on the survey findings. Health Canada funds the Brighter Futures Program, which works under the Health Department. The main goal is to educate and help Algonquins of all ages stay healthy and active.

Sitting on the Fence

Youth living on the Akwesasne Mohawk Reservation live in the extreme northeast section of the United States and the extreme southeastern section of Canada; the reservation is on the border of both countries, and students can choose whether they want to attend a Canadian school or a U.S. school. (People living on the reserve do not have to go through *customs* every time they cross into the other country.) The elementary and middle-school students can also choose between the Mohawk school on Cornwall Island or the local public schools. High school students can choose between the Canadian high school or the nearby American high school. "Most kids go to the school that is closest to them," says Karen Gravelle, author of *Soaring Spirits: Conversations with Native American Teens*.

Richard Point attended the Mohawk school and liked it a lot. Although it was in Canada, the school had different classes from other Canadian schools. Instead of taking French, they studied Mohawk. Stacey Montour also attended the school, and her favorite

Many Native teens face stereotypes and prejudice. Studying and learning together helps them form a strong sense of identity to help them overcome this challenge.

class was Mohawk. She is not fluent yet but she can understand what people are saying when they speak in Mohawk. Connie Oaks attended a public school in New York State.

Karen Gravelle writes that Connie, Stacey, and Richard all believe that "many white kids see them in a negative way, and this hurts and angers them. 'People over there don't know that we're almost the same,' Richard says. 'They think we're a lot different than they are. We're supposed to be dressed up in feathers, you know.'

"'They probably think we're really mean, but we're not bad people!' Connie adds."

Like on other reserves, many high school students do not finish school. When a person does not feel welcome at a school, it is harder to stay put and finish. The three friends knew many students who had already dropped out of school.

School is important in the lives of all North American teenagers. For youth growing up on reservations and among First Nation communities, education is particularly important. It can help them connect successfully with the culture beyond their own communities, enabling them to lead productive lives as adults. For Native communities, however, the challenge is to make sure that at the same time, schools affirm rather than erode their unique traditions and heritage.

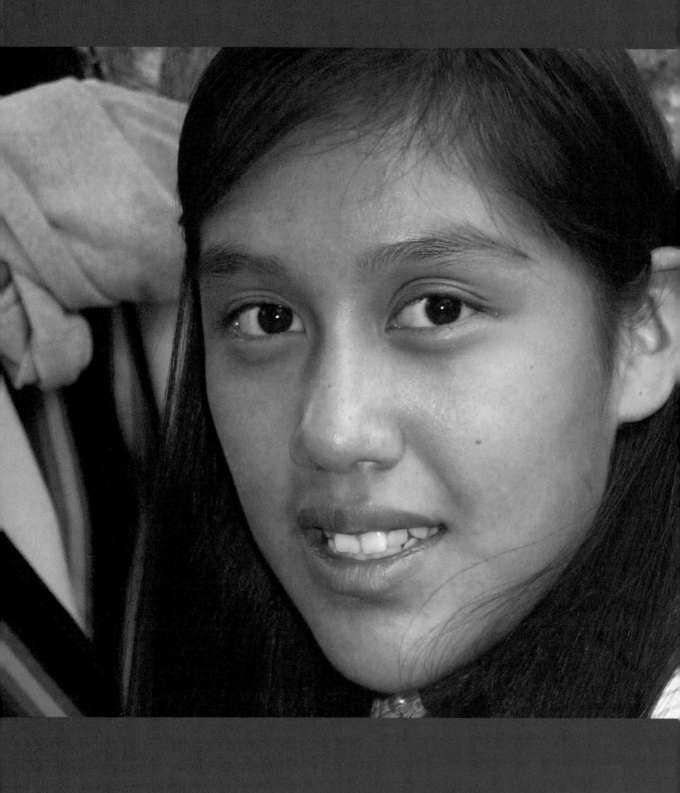

CHAPTER 7
Challenges and Hopes for the Future

"Look around your community, find a problem, and solve it." This was the challenge given to teens around the United States by a national science competition. Four girls on the Crow Reservation—Lucretia Birdinground, Kimberly Deputee, Omney Sees The Ground, and Brennet Stewart—accepted the challenge. Lucretia remembers the day when she was in eighth grade that their science teacher and coach, Jack Joyce, talked with each girl individually and encouraged them all to get involved with the exciting national science competition.

Growing up on isolated rural reservations like this one presents a number of challenges for Native teens—but many of them are finding creative solutions for their people's problems.

The girls looked around the Crow Reservation and observed that lack of housing was one problem touching many people. Families were crowded together with other families in a single house. Jobs were hard to find on the reservation, and housing was scarce—but families continued to live there, not wanting to move away from relatives. The girls interviewed these families and found that one of the problems caused by overcrowding was that children had no quiet place to study and do their homework.

They had identified a problem; now it was time to find a solution. Their first task was to name themselves. They decided they'd be the Rez Protectors.

With a little help from their science teacher, they realized that one thing the community had much of was hay. Couldn't this be used somehow to build houses? Mr. Joyce told the girls there was a way to build houses out of hay bales covered with a mixture of lime, cement, and sand. The girls talked with many people who were skeptical about the project, but they went ahead anyway.

First, they tested to see whether water would leak into the hay bales when it rained. Then they used a torch and thermometer to prove that the bales would be heat-proof and fireproof. Their tests showed that hay could be a good building material.

Now the Rez Protectors had to write a ten-page paper describing the problem, the anticipated answer, the tests performed, and the results. They also had to write about what they would do for the community if they won the prize of $25,000. The girls decided they would build a hay-bale community study hall for Crow students. This would give students from crowded homes a quiet place to study.

The Rez Protectors were one of the top-ten teams chosen to go to Orlando, Florida, to spend a week at Disney World. They had placed above five hundred other teams. While presenting their project in Florida, the girls wore their Crow traditional dresses and were awarded the best-dressed team on the last night at the awards banquet. At the end of the evening, the judges made the announcement: the Rez Protectors won first place!

The Crow community helped build the hay-bale study hall, and the girls were celebrities on *Oprah*. Tom Brokaw and the *Today Show* interviewed them, and Al Gore invited the Rez Protectors to his Family Reunion Conference, where Lucretia spoke to five hundred people. The team hopes that housing will not be such a problem in the future for the Crow Nation, and that their hay-bale house project will catch the interest of people on the reservation.

Family

Lucretia Birdinground speaks fondly of the encouragement her family gave her for the hay-bale project. They have always been there for her in other situations as well. She laughingly says that her family is just like the family in the movie, *My Big Fat Greek Wedding*: they are always around trying to help and be a part of things. Her grandfather, Glen Birdinground, has had a particularly deep influence on her. He was confined to a wheelchair for many years, but he did not let that stop him from becoming a tribal judge. He spent much time with Lucretia and her brother and always encouraged them to make good choices in life and to do the right thing. Because of his influence, Lucretia wants to become a lawyer.

A wall covered with family photos is a common sight in the homes of Native American families. Children's school photos, along with photos taken at sports events and on special occasions, are on the wall for all visitors to see. The Allen Curley family on the Navajo nation is no exception: their living room wall is covered with photos—from his oldest daughter, Nicole, who is involved in ROTC and sports; to his son, Nicholas, a football and basketball player; to Trisha Ann, who is a basketball and track team member, and a National American Miss Pageant contestant. Just looking around the home tells visitors how important family is to the Curleys.

Trisha credits her sister Nicole as the role model who inspires her constantly. "She is in ROTC, she stays out of trouble, she gets awards

Family plays an important role in the lives of many Native young adults.

for everything she does, she is an honor student, she is in National Honor Society, and she does everything with me."

Meanwhile, many uncles and cousins have influenced her brother Nicholas. When hunting season comes, they all hunt together. They share ideas and techniques for tracking down deer. They stick together and learn from each other.

Families are the most important influence in the lives of young people. From our families we learn our sense of right and wrong; we learn how we fit into the world; we gain an understanding of life and religion. Family has always been particularly important to Native people, and it will continue to be important if language and traditions are to survive.

Language

When asked about the number of Navajos who speak their own language, Allen Curley believes the children who speak Navajo only do so because the parents and grandparents have intentionally spoken it at home: if parents do not push their native language at home, the children will not learn the language.

The problem of keeping Native language alive is a common one for North American Indians. As the older generations die, it becomes increasingly difficult to find individuals who are fluent in their own tongue. Native young people are growing up in two worlds: the world of CDs, the Internet, and TV; and the world of their Native identity. If they lose their language, then they will lose the vocabulary that will allow them to shape the thoughts and values that are essential to their culture. That's why preserving their language is a priority for many Native groups.

Other Important Issues

A healthy lifestyle is important to the well-being of any person, people, and nation. Canadian Aboriginal youth are the largest group of young people in Canada, so how they take care of their health and well-being will affect not only their First Nations communities but also the entire country.

The National Aboriginal Health Organization (NAHO) is an organization dedicated to developing good health among First Nation members. At the North American Indigenous Games in Winnipeg, Manitoba, in 2002, Jason Whitebear, who works for NAHO, gathered information on health priorities and general youth issues from athletes. He found that when it came to health matters, they were the most concerned about the use of alcohol, drugs, tobacco, and the high suicide rate among Aboriginal teens. They were also concerned about teen pregnancy and sexually transmitted disease. Under the category of general youth issues, most of the athletes felt that education, racism, and gangs were the biggest concerns. A lack of activities available in their communities and domestic violence were also issues.

The youth surveyed had suggestions on what would best help Aboriginal youth. They would like to see more recreational facilities with more sports available, and more interaction with elders, listening to their stories and teachings on tradition. They suggested more activities with a youth focus, workshops and conferences on health issues, and improved educational services. The youth felt they needed more role models and more parent and community involvement in their activities. Many of them thought that a revival of Aboriginal culture and use of Aboriginal languages in the classroom would be helpful. Some suggested that better relations between Aboriginal and non-Aboriginal people would be beneficial.

Whitebear discovered that most of his interviewees did not see health as fun. He concluded that community workers were going to have to work hard to encourage healthy lifestyles and healthy living. They need to make health enjoyable and interesting to the youth. Trust is an important factor; once the youth see the community worker as one of them, then they will listen and respect what they have to say.

One of the biggest challenges of belonging to a First Nations community or on an Indian reservation arises when the time comes to leave, whether for college or to get a job. Native students are choosing Indian colleges in large numbers, but some are interested in degrees that only state colleges can give. According to a recent report, the number of Native Americans going to higher education institutions jumped from 76,000 to 127,000 in 2004.

American Indian Report, November 2004, says that Native youth who attend universities face many challenges. Nickole Fox, a student and member of University of Michigan's Native American Student Association (NASA), says that some non-Indian people have no idea of what it's like to be an Indian student at a mainstream university. "They think Native people aren't around anymore, and are, maybe, surprised when we speak up." Indian students report dealing with ignorance and racism in many classrooms. Sometimes Native students encounter societies that used Indian names and rituals. The University of Michigan had such a group, the "Tribe of Michigamua." The club has since dropped the name and their rituals, but some Native students wonder if it secretly still uses in them.

It can be difficult for students to leave their close-knit communities. Homesickness can be a real problem, but more students than ever are sticking it out and graduating. Fox said that it is important to find a Native American support group, just as she did with NASA. These groups can be a tremendous help in making a person feel more at home.

Drugs are another issue Native youths must face. Shirley Watkins, the Tobacco Education Prevention Program coordinator on the Navajo Reservation, says her group is trying to stop the use of drugs by nipping in the bud a lesser problem—tobacco use. If they can stop cigarette smoking before kids start the habit, then perhaps they have a better chance of eliminating drugs such as marijuana, the leading drug on the Navajo reservation, and the new runner-up, crystal methamphetamine (meth). Meth is growing in popularity because it is powerful and cheap, but unfortunately, it is highly addictive.

Meth has come to many rural areas in recent years, so it is not surprising that it has made its way onto reservations in the United States and Canada. Officials are offering new drug treatment programs in Regina, Saskatchewan. *Newsweek* magazine states that meth use at U.S. Indian Health Service sites has gone from 2,176 in all of 2000 to 4,077 in early September 2004. Non-Indian and Indian traffickers are targeting even very remote reservations, since drug sellers believe not as many police watch such areas.

The Navajo nation outlawed the use of methamphetamine on the reservation in February of 2005. Until then, officials had not de-

Native teens face many challenges—but with help from their communities, they can find the strength, pride, and ingenuity to rise above them.

clared it illegal, but now it is punishable by up to a year in jail or a $5,000 fine. Problems that have always existed on many reservations—such as poverty, alcoholism, and a high unemployment rate—have kept officials busy enough that they were slow to realize the meth problem was rising. The Navajo Behavioral Health staff is using traditional methods such as sweat lodges and other traditions, along with Western medicine, to fight addiction.

Home, in many Native communities, is both a beautiful and difficult place to live. Todd Wilkinson, a correspondent for the *Christian Science Monitor*, writes that Indian teens live closer to tragedy than most other teens. Poverty on reservations is a problem, along with alcoholism, single-parent households, teenage pregnancy, and physical abuse. The percentage of males who die before age thirty is higher than it is for the general public.

Walking on the *Hozhoogo Naashaa*—what the Navajo call the Beauty Way, the path of health and beauty—while living in First Nation communities and on Native American reservations can be both a challenge and a joy. These communities are places where people have the same ethnicity and kinship, the same history, language, and traditions. They are places where, as Monty Roessel says, "we can be with people to whom we go first when we need comfort or empathy, for they speak our own brand of cultural shorthand, and always know the correct things to say, the proper things to do."

The Blessed Beauty Way

Great Spirit, may I walk in Beauty!
May Beauty be above me,
So that I may be a part of the Greater Beauty.
Great Spirit, may I walk in Beauty.
May Beauty be in front of me,
That I may perceive Beauty in all things.
Great Spirit, may I walk in Beauty.
May Beauty be to the left of me,
That I may receive Beauty through my inner woman.
Great Spirit, may I walk in Beauty.
May Beauty be to the right of me,
That I may give Beauty through my inner man.
Great Spirit, may I walk in Beauty.
May Beauty be behind me,
So that the only tracks I leave are those of Beauty.
Great Spirit, may I walk in Beauty.
May I touch my self, my life, and all others with Beauty.
May I walk this Blessed Beauty Way.
Great Spirit, may I walk in Beauty.

—a Navajo prayer

Further Reading

Ancona, George. *Earth Daughter: Alicia of Acoma Pueblo*. New York: Simon and Shuster Books for Young Readers, 1995.

Colton, Larry. *Counting Coup: A True Story of Basketball and Honor on the Little Big Horn*. New York: Warner Books, Inc., 2000.

Franco, Betsy, Traci L. Gourdine, and Annette Pina Ochoa (editors). *Night Is Gone, Day Is Still Coming*. Cambridge, Mass.: Candlewick Press, 2003.

Gravelle, Karen. *Soaring Spirits: Conversations with Native American Teens*. Lincoln, Neb.: Authors Guild, 2000.

Kavasch, E. Barrie. *Zuni Children and Elders Talk Together*. New York: Rosen Publishing Group, Inc., 1999.

Locke, Raymond Friday. *The Book of the Navajo*. Los Angeles: Mankind Publishing Company, 2001.

McIntosh, Kenneth. *North American Indians Today: Crow*. Broomall, Pa.: Mason Crest Publishers, 2004.

Roessel, Monty. *Kinaalda: A Navajo Girl Grows Up*. Minneapolis, Minn.: Lerner Publishing, 2000.

Stewart, Phillip. *North American Indians Today: Osage*. Broomall, Pa.: Mason Crest Publishers, 2004.

Tremble, Stephen. *The People: Indians of the American Southwest*. Santa Fe, N.M.: School of American Research Press, 2003.

For More Information

Alternet
www.alternet.org

Carlisle Indian School
members.tripod.com/~johnnyrodgers/centralsqindian.html

Dine Woven
dinewoven.com

Indianz.com
www.indianz.com/News/2004/002770.asp

National Aboriginal Health Organization
www.naho.ca/firstnations/english/welcome_page.php

Native Voices Foundation
www.nativevoices.org/articles/chance_for_hope.htm

Powwow Trail
www.powersource.com/gallery/powwow/question.html

Rodeo Introduction
www.civilization.ca/aborig/rodeo/rodeo05e.html

The Society of St. Francis
In Beauty We Walk: The Spirituality of the Navajo Indians
www.franciscans.org.uk/1999sep-pamelaclarecsf.html

Publisher's note:
The Web sites listed on this page were active at the time of publication. The publisher is not responsible for Web sites that have changed their addresses or discontinued operation since the date of publication. The publisher will review and update the Web-site list upon each reprint.

Glossary

breaking: Training a horse to accept a harness, saddle, bit, and rider.

concho: A Native American ornamental disk (as on clothing or a tack) featuring a shell or flower design.

customs: The agency or procedure for collecting duties or tolls imposed by the law of a country on imports or exports.

Four Corners: The location where the states of Colorado, New Mexico, Arizona, and Utah meet.

fry bread: A quick bread cooked by deep-frying.

homesteading: The claiming of land by a settler or squatter under terms of the U.S. Homestead Act ore the Canadian Dominion Lands Act.

Indian agent: A representative of the U.S. government to the Native American community.

indigenous: Native to an area.

medicine man: A priestly healer.

mesas: Isolated, relatively flat-topped natural elevations, usually larger than a butte and smaller than a plateau.

powwow: North American Indian social gathering or fair that usually includes competitive dancing.

regalia: Special dress or finery.

secular: Not controlled by a religious body or concerned with religious or spiritual matters.

sovereign nations: Governments with the authority over their own laws and people.

tract: An unmeasured area of land.

tripe: Stomach lining of an animal, used for food.

washes: Dry stream beds.

Bibliography

Alberta Government, International, Intergovernmental and Aboriginal Relation
http://www.aand.gov.ab.ca/AANDNonFlash/9272E0671503486DA4EF4FE4A1E7D
3BA_071F73CE0928474897D13E76007A1372.htm.

Bureau of Indian Affairs
http://www.doi.gov/bureau-indian-affairs.html.

Colton, Larry. *Counting Coup: A True Story of Basketball and Honor on the Little Big Horn*. New York: Warner Books, 2000.

First Perspective, National Aboriginal News
http://www.firstperspective.ca.

McIntosh, Kenneth. *North American Indians Today: Crow*. Broomall, Pa.: Mason Crest Publishers, 2004.

Reyhner, Jon Allan. *Teaching American Indian Students*. Norman, OK.: University of Oklahoma Press, 1994.

Trimble, Stephen. *The People: Indians of the American Southwest*. Santa Fe, NM.: School of American Research Press, 1993.

United States Department of the Interior Library
http://library.doi.gov/internet/native.html.

Wagner, Katherine. *The Way People Live – Life on an Indian Reservation*. Farmington Hills, Mich.: Lucent Books, 2004.

Index

Picture Credits

Harding House Publishing, Ben Stewart: pp. 31, 63, 65, 69, 70, 73, 74, 76, 78
iStockphoto:
   Allegra, Marisa: p. 15
   Gingerich, Andrea: pp. 26, 50
   Monino, Juan: pp. 12, 46
   Morgan, Ryan: p. 53
   Parkin, Jim: pp. 23, 49
   Stephens, Jacom: p. 44
   Svetlana, Larina: p. 33
   Zhenikeyev, Arman: p. 25
   Zierlein, Frank: p. 11
Library of Congress: p. 54
McIntosh, Kenneth: pp. 8, 17, 18, 21, 28, 32, 36, 39, 40, 43, 56, 59, 60, 66, 80, 83, 87

To the best knowledge of the publisher, all other images are in the public domain. If any image has been inadvertently uncredited, please notify Harding House Publishing Service, Vestal, New York 13850, so that rectification can be made for future printings.

Biographies

Author

Marsha McIntosh is a freelance writer living in Flagstaff, Arizona. She was an elementary teacher for nine years and taught in the Migrant Workers Tutorial Program in St. Paul, Minnesota. As the Assistant Coordinator for the CASS program in Upstate New York, she worked with college students from Central America and the Caribbean. She was a researcher and co-author of several books in the Mason Crest series NORTH AMERICAN INDIANS TODAY. She enjoys living in northern Arizona with its mix of Hispanic and American Indian cultures.

Series Consultant

Celeste J. Carmichael is a 4-H Youth Development Program Specialist at the Cornell University Cooperative Extension Administrative Unit in Ithaca, New York. She provides leadership to statewide 4-H Youth Development efforts including communications, curriculum, and conferences. She communicates the needs and impacts of the 4-H program to staff and decision makers, distributing information about issues related to youth and development, such as trends for rural youth.